Three Together

igloo

Published in 2008
by Igloo Books Ltd
Cottage Farm,
Sywell,
NN6 0BJ
www.igloo-books.com

10 9 8 7 6 5 4 3 2 1

ISBN: 978 1 84561 929 9

Cover design by Insight Design
Cover illustrated by © Rachel Ellen Designs Ltd
Interior illustrations by Liz and Kate Pope

Printed and manufactured in China

The Mystery of the Missing Map

by Carol Lawrence

igloo

Chapter 1

The Mysterious Notes

"Come on, you two. We're going to get locked in if we don't hurry!" Poppy called. Poppy was nine, with jet-black hair and bright green eyes that sparkled. She, KC and Sam had spent almost the whole day in the museum, and they'd had a great time. The museum was full of old statues, spooky-looking paintings, and ancient armour and clothes. Today was a school visit, and everyone else was ready to leave.

"We're coming!" KC shouted back to Poppy. KC was Poppy's best friend.

KC and Poppy told each other everything. Everything, that is, except for one thing: what the initials KC stood for! Whenever anyone asked her, KC giggled. Poppy thought it was great to have a friend with such a cool secret.

"What's the hurry?" Sam ran up to them with his camera. Sam was Poppy's seven-and-a-half-year old brother. He liked taking pictures that he could download to his computer at home. Sam had taken photographs of everything he'd seen. "I took a picture of an old owl in a case, and a cool sword, and a fossil of a fish," said Sam. "I love this place!" His voice echoed down the dusty halls.

Poppy looked around while Sam and KC were checking to be sure they had all their things. She could see a display of stuffed birds that glared with glass eyes, a shield in the corner with the lions on, and . . . what was that?

She ran across the room and picked up something from the floor. Just a bit of paper. Poppy unfolded it, and read,

TO FIND THE MAP, GO THROUGH THE ARCH

Poppy looked around. Apart from KC, Sam, and her teacher Mrs. Oates, there was no one else in the room. Poppy showed the note to KC and Sam. "What do you think this means?"

They shrugged, but Poppy was thinking fast. Poppy liked a lot of things – swimming, bike riding, reading and playing sports – but there was one thing Poppy liked most of all: solving mysteries. And this looked like a mystery.

There was only one thing to do. Poppy went through the brick arch and into the corridor, with KC and Sam following. The corridor seemed to go on forever. As they walked, the lights were turned off so they could only see a little way ahead.

"Poppy, this is weird," said KC. She didn't like surprises or spookiness, and she really didn't like the dark.

"Why would anyone leave a note like that?" wondered Sam. Unusual or mysterious things annoyed him.

They reached a crossroads with a large statue of a man with a spear.

Poppy spotted something white on the floor by

the statue. Another note? She picked it up.

TAKE THE SECOND TURN UP AHEAD

She could hear Mrs. Oates calling, "Come on! We're leaving right away!"

"Quick! We have to find out what's going on," Poppy said, and started to run.

Another note on the floor!

THE MAP IS ON THE FAR WALL IN THE NEXT ROOM. YOU DON'T HAVE MUCH TIME.

The friends rushed around the corner into a little room that looked as though it was never used. The walls were bare, except for one frame on the wall opposite them.

But the frame was empty. Poppy heard the sound of clattering footsteps, and a stern-looking

woman came in. "I'm Mrs. MacArthur, the museum curator. Why are you children still in here?"

Poppy pointed to the wall. "Excuse me, is there meant to be a map there?"

Mrs. MacArthur looked at the frame. "Why, yes, there is. Where is it?" She peered at the three friends over her glasses. Even though they hadn't done anything wrong, it was hard not to feel guilty.

"We don't know," said Poppy. "We just followed these clues, and the map wasn't here!"

The friends tried to explain about the paper clues to Mrs. MacArthur, but she wasn't listening. "That map," she said, as if she was giving a lesson, "is the floor plan to Lyon Place. We only moved the map into this room today. You know Lyon Place?"

KC nodded. "It's the really big old house, just down the street."

"Correct," Mrs. MacArthur said. "The map was probably taken down for cleaning, though I should have been told. And now, children, would you kindly leave the building? It's three minutes after closing time!"

"But —" Mrs. MacArthur was already striding off, and wasn't listening to Poppy at all. Poppy sighed, and stuffed the pieces of paper in her backpack.

"Don't mind her," said a deep voice from behind them. "She has a lot on her mind. Not much time for anything!"

At first, the friends thought a statue was walking out of the dark alcove behind them. It was a tall, thin figure wearing a peaked cap. But as the figure came into the light, they realised it was an elderly man in a uniform.

"Mr. Grant's the name," he said. "Security guard for the museum." He twitched his grey moustache.

"You scared us a little," said KC. "We thought you were an exhibit."

Mr. Grant laughed, and even his laugh was a little dry and dusty. "Sometimes I feel like one, too!"

"Mr. Grant," said Poppy, "What's happened to the map, the one that was in that frame?"

The security guard looked at the empty frame. "I don't know," he said. "It was in the frame ten minutes ago. But if Mrs. MacArthur says it was taken away to be cleaned, she must be right. I'll go check. And now it's time you were hurrying along. Museum's closed!" Mr. Grant led them back to the main entrance.

The three friends travelled home on the school bus, then walked to Poppy and Sam's house.

"That was weird," said Sam. "I didn't like that curer woman!"

"Curator," said Poppy. "That's what the person who organizes a museum is called."

"Why would someone leave a trail of clues to reach a map?" asked KC. "A map that isn't even there?"

"I don't know," said Poppy. "It's a real mystery. And I think that map hasn't just been taken down to be cleaned. I think it's been stolen! Even Mr. Grant, that nice security guard, thought it was, really. He just didn't want to disagree with Mrs. MacArthur."

KC and Sam agreed.

"Look," said Poppy, pointing across the road. "That street leads to Lyon Place, the house that was on the map. Let's go see what it looks like!"

Poppy, KC and Sam took the turning into the street. It was full of big, sprawling houses with long paths across wide lawns. Everything looked clean and ordered. "Wow," said Sam. "You could put six of our house into one of these!"

Lyon Place was at the end of the street. But it wasn't at all like the others. It was even bigger, but its grey stone was crumbling and the curtains in the windows looked faded and old. Even the white paint on the front door was peeling.

"Someone needs to fix up this house," said KC. "Imagine what it must be like inside. It's probably got more awesome old stuff in it than the museum."

As they watched, Poppy saw the curtains of one of the top windows twitch. "Somebody knows we're looking!" she said.

A small, pale hand drew back the curtains, and a small, pale face gazed out. It was the face of a little girl, about Poppy and KC's age. Then it saw them!

For a second, Poppy felt scared, as if she wanted to run. But the pale face smiled. Without thinking, Poppy waved. Slowly, the little girl raised her hand and waved back. Then she turned from the window, as if she could hear someone speaking to her. She moved away, and the faded red curtains fell back.

The friends looked at each other in surprise.

"Hmm," said Poppy as they walked back down the street. "That was just as exciting as a missing map – and just as mysterious!"

Chapter 2

The Girl in the Window

The next day was a school day, and Poppy and KC didn't have much time to talk about strange clues, the map or the girl in the house. When it was time for lunch, they found Sam coming out of his classroom

"I'm starving," he moaned. Poppy and KC laughed. Sam always seemed to be hungry!

"Let's go to the canteen," said Poppy, and they set off.

"What's that noise?" asked KC. They could hear shouting and laughing coming from around the corner. Not nice laughing, but a cruel, teasing kind of laughter.

"Sounds like Luke and Lucy," said Poppy, frowning.

Luke and Lucy were twins. Lucy always wanted to be the best at everything, and Luke did whatever Lucy told him. Sure enough, when they turned the corner they saw that Luke and Lucy had cornered a smaller girl and were laughing at her.

"You only come here because you have to, now!" said Luke. He was the biggest boy in his class, and nobody could beat him in sports. He had closely-cropped hair that stuck out from his head.

"Yes," said Lucy, her ponytail wagging as she pushed at the person in front of her, who was hidden by Luke's bulk. "Go back to your stupid old school. You don't belong here!"

Poppy wasn't scared of Luke or Lucy. She walked up to them and stood in front of the small girl they were bullying. "Leave her alone," she told them, "or I'll tell the headmaster, and I'll also tell her about the time you went on the ghost train at the fair and came out crying!"

Luke and Lucy's sneer disappeared and they looked worried. "That ghost train was really scary," he said. "It had three skeletons in it!"

"Come on, Luke," Lucy said, dragging him away. "Let's go outside."

Poppy turned to see girl they'd been bothering. "I'm sorry," she said. "Not everyone here is like that. It's —" Poppy stopped as she recognised the girl's small, pale face and the cloud of fair hair around it. It was the girl from the window at Lyon Place.

"I know you," said the girl. "You were outside my window."

"Um, yes we were," said Poppy quietly. It was hard to know what to say without looking weird. "We wanted to see what your house looks like."

The girl suddenly looked sad. "It won't be my house for much longer. My family has to sell the house."

"Come have lunch with us," KC invited. Tell us all about it!"

So they all sat down in the hall and heard her story.

"My name's Olivia," said the girl. "Olivia Lyon. My family has lived in Lyon Place for just about forever. My ancestor actually built it, long ago. But now we don't have any money. That's why I'm starting school here. My old private school cost too much."

"This school is pretty cool," said Sam. "Apart from Luke and Lucy, everybody's really nice."

Olivia smiled. "That's good. I think I'll be here for a long time. My dad is selling Lyon Place, and we have to move out in about a week." She tried not to show it, but the friends could see that Olivia was very upset.

Poppy remembered the missing map. "The reason we were outside your house," she said, "was because we think someone stole a map of your house from the museum." She told Olivia what had happened yesterday.

Olivia's eyes widened. "You're detectives?" she asked. "That's so great! I bet you could find that missing map if you wanted to!"

Poppy nodded. "We've found some stuff for people before."

"Why don't you come over to Lyon Place tonight?" suggested Olivia. "That way, you can see it before it's gone."

Now it was the friends' turn to be excited. "Can

we really?" Poppy said. "Yes, we'll definitely come over!" They all wanted to know what the old mansion was like inside.

After school, Poppy, Sam and KC rushed to their homes to get permission to go to Olivia's house. It wasn't long before they were standing outside Lyon Place again. Only this time, they were about to go in.

Poppy stepped up and pressed the big, rusty doorbell. A giant clanging sound echoed from deep in the house and, suddenly, the friends felt the tiniest bit scared.

Chapter 3

Inside Lyon Place

"I wonder if a spooky old butler will open the door," Poppy wondered to herself, as the friends waited outside Lyon Place.

But, when the door opened, it was Olivia standing there. "Hi! Come in."

Poppy, KC and Sam found themselves standing in a wide hall painted in a pale, faded blue. An old chandelier hung from the high ceiling and, at the back, a giant staircase curled its way upstairs.

Olivia's mum came into the hall. She was a tall, smiling woman. "Pleased to meet you all," she said. "Before you see the house, would anyone like a snack?"

They followed Olivia and her mum to the gigantic kitchen and munched happily away on some delicious, chocolate chip cookies.

"I baked them myself," said Olivia's mum. "I guess it's the last bit of baking I'll be able to do here. We're moving the stove and the fridge out in a day or two. So, it'll be take-away pizzas until the end of the week for you, Olivia!"

"Wow," Sam said, splattering cookie crumbs. "I wish I got to eat pizza every day!"

Olivia took them up the massive winding staircase to the upper floor. Although everything was very old, and some of the corners were a little dusty, everything the friends saw made them stare. There were candlestick holders on the walls, huge mirrors on the walls, and vases big enough for Sam to hide in.

At the end of the upstairs hall hung a huge painting, towering over everything else. It showed a man in a three-cornered hat and red beard that reached down almost to his knees. He was smiling

grimly, showing a gold tooth. The painting looked old, but the man looked very much alive. He was surrounded by piles of big gold coins. And he looked as if there was an enormous joke that only he knew.

"Who's that?" asked Poppy. "He looks really scary!"

"That's my great-great-great-great-great-great-grandfather," said Olivia. "Charlie Lyon."

"Oops!" said Poppy. "I'm sorry."

"That's okay," smiled Olivia. "He was really scary. Charlie Lyon was a ferocious pirate, hundreds of years ago. He got all that gold by stealing it from ships that were taking it across the sea. They used to call him Crossbones Charlie."

"Oooh," said KC, looking closely at Olivia. "So you're actually descended from a real-life pirate?"

Olivia grinned and nodded. "Arrr, me hearties!"

They all laughed, but it was strange thinking that the man in the picture was really related to the little blonde girl right in front of them.

"When he had all the gold he wanted, he built Lyon Place. Lyons have lived here ever since. Until now," said Olivia sadly. "Anyway, come on. I want to show you the nursery!"

She led them into a big room that was as faded as the others. The floor was strewn with all kinds of toys and clothes. All of them looked very old, and very unusual. None of the friends had seen anything like it before.

"They used to call this room the nursery," Olivia explained. "It was the room for very little children. I don't sleep in here, but I still play in here."

KC stroked a rocking horse. Poppy spotted an old white dress with a beautiful blue ribbon around it. Sam picked up a funny tin robot with a key in the back. He wound it up and watched as the robot lurched across the floor.

"You're so lucky to have all these toys!" said Poppy, saying what they all felt.

Olivia shrugged. "Most of it's too damaged to sell. Dad says we'll probably have to give it to charity when we move. The new house is too small to keep. Go on Poppy, try on the dress!"

Soon all of them were trying on the strange old clothes.

Poppy put on the white dress. "I feel like Alice in Wonderland," she said.

KC found a brilliant purple dress that reached right down to the floor.

Sam found a little black suit, complete with a top hat. "Excellent," he said. "I want to wear a top hat every day!"

Olivia's mum appeared at the door. "Everything okay?"

Olivia nodded.

"Well, have fun. Just don't go treasure hunting again, Olivia!"

Olivia's mum went back downstairs, and Olivia blushed. "There's an old legend that Crossbones Charlie left a big pile of gold hidden somewhere in the house. People have searched everywhere for years and years, but nobody's ever found it. So everyone thinks it's just a story."

"Do you think it's just a story?" asked Poppy in excitement.

"I don't know. I always look for it when I can. The other day I went right up to the attic and searched but I almost fell down the ladder and Mum was very cross. She doesn't want me looking again."

It was strange to be dressed in old clothes, talking about finding a real life pirate treasure. "A bit like time traveling," thought Poppy.

They took the clothes off carefully and went back downstairs to eat. Poppy couldn't help looking at all the doors, walls and paintings. What if that painting opened up and revealed the treasure? Did that bookcase have a hidden lever that opened a door to a secret treasure room? She was looking so hard, she nearly tripped.

After they'd said goodbye, Poppy, KC and Sam walked back to KC's house, where the friends parted for the night.

As they reached their house and went upstairs, Poppy couldn't stop thinking about the treasure. And Sam couldn't stop talking about it. "I bet it's all true," he said. "I'm going to look it up on the computer right now."

"Sam, it's very late," said Mum. "Don't be long!"

Soon, Sam was searching. "Look!" he said before long. "Crossbones Charlie!" The screen showed a picture of him, looking very fierce. He had a curved sword between his teeth, and he was swinging from a rope onto a ship.

"It says here that Crossbones Charlie Lyon was the most dangerous pirate on the High Seas. His motto was 'Never surrender.' He built Lyon Place and the old town hall," read Sam. "The old town hall is now the museum. Hey, Poppy, he built the museum too!"

"Wow," said Poppy. "Is there anything about the treasure?"

"Hmm . . . let's see . . . it says that, although he spent lots of money, he kept most of it somewhere where it would never be found. And, when he died, his family looked everywhere but they couldn't find it. Now, people think it was Charlie's joke, to annoy his family."

Poppy remembered Crossbones Charlie's grim smile on the painting. He looked like somebody who might do that. But maybe the treasure really was still in Lyon Place.

Sam said, "If only there was a clue. Directions or . . ." Sam and Poppy looked at each other.

"A map!" they said at the same time.

"Maybe someone has taken the map from the museum to help them find the treasure," said Sam. "That's got to be it."

"If we can find the map," said Poppy, "we can find the treasure!"

Chapter 4
Hunting for Treasure

It seemed like ages before Poppy could sit down with Sam, KC and Olivia at lunch the next day. "We don't care what the grown ups say," Poppy told her friends. "We think the treasure is real. And, imagine, Olivia; if you find the pirate treasure, your family will have so much money that you won't have to move out of Lyon Place!"

Olivia looked excited. "Is it true? You really think so?"

"We're excellent at detecting," Poppy said. "We'll find the gold. If only we can work out where the map has gone, then we can use it to find the treasure."

"But that map is very old," said Olivia. "Wouldn't someone have noticed a secret on it by now?"

"Maybe not," said Poppy, confidently. "Maybe nobody's looked at the map because it's been in the museum for so long."

"It doesn't matter anyway," said Olivia, with a far-away look in her eyes. "Next week, Lyon Place won't belong to my family any more."

"That doesn't mean we should give up," said KC excitedly. "We've still got a few days to find the treasure. We should start by going back to the museum tomorrow after school, to find out if the map is really missing. Maybe they've found it, and they'll let us see it!"

"Treasure?" said a voice from behind them. Not a nice voice. "What treasure?"

It was Luke and Lucy. Luke stood behind them, towering over them as they sat at the table. Lucy looked down her nose at them. "Come on," she said. "Tell us all about it."

"We want some treasure, too!" said Luke.

"It's none of your business," said Poppy, bravely. "We're having a private discussion."

"Oh, really? We're making it our business, too!" said Lucy. She motioned to Luke, and they walked off.

"What did they mean?" asked Olivia, worried.

"Oh, don't worry about those two," said Sam,

stronger than he felt. "They always want to mess up other people's plans."

"Our first step is to go back to the museum," said Poppy. "Let's ask our parents if we can go tomorrow after school!"

"I can't," said Olivia. "I have to pack up my stuff for the move. Can you all look without me?"

"No problem," said Poppy. "We're on the case!"

As Poppy and KC walked back to class, they saw Luke and Lucy slip out to the schoolyard. "Quick," said Poppy. "Let's follow them and find out what they're planning!"

"I don't know, Poppy," said KC. "What if they see us?"

"Don't worry," said Poppy. "They won't!"

She took KC's hand and they crept up to the door that led outside.

"We can hear what they're saying from here."

The two friends crouched down under the frosted window. If they looked through, they could see the silhouettes of the twins – one large, one thin. When Poppy pressed her ear against the wall, she could hear them, too.

"I'm going to buy the fastest sports car," said Luke.

"Don't be an idiot, you can't drive," said Lucy, in her familiar sneering tone. "I'm going to buy jewels and a big gold crown. And a pony and a boat and a butler, and new teachers that will tell me I'm right all the time!"

Poppy leaned over to KC. "They're talking about the treasure!"

KC nodded. She was still worried that they'd be caught.

"I don't think you can buy teachers," said Luke, uncertainly. "No matter how much treasure you have. I'd pay them lots of money to go away, though."

"Shut up, idiot," said Lucy. "We need to get into that stupid old house. That must be where the treasure is hidden."

"How are we going to do that?" asked Luke.

At that moment, Poppy tried to shift her weight and slipped slightly. She grabbed KC before she could fall and almost toppled them both.

"What was that?" Lucy said, suddenly sounding

suspicious. "Come on, idiot! Someone might be listening!"

As Luke and Lucy went back to the door, Poppy and KC stood up. There wasn't any time to make a run for it. The only other door was on the other side of the room. They were trapped, and there was nothing they could do!

Lucy pushed the door open. KC and Poppy stood behind it, trying to be silent. Lucy didn't see them hiding behind the door.

"Let's go," Lucy said. "We're going to be late for class."

They walked slowly out of the room. As they reached the other side, Lucy looked back, but there was nobody there.

She sniffed and pushed Luke out of the room, following him.

From the schoolyard, Poppy and KC let out long sighs of relief. "Good thing we crept out here while their backs

were turned," said Poppy, grinning. "Or they'd have seen us for sure! Admit it, KC, that was pretty exciting!"

KC nodded. "I guess. Let's just not do it again, okay?"

The friends met up again at the end of school. Poppy saw Olivia running to meet her mum outside the gates. Olivia's mum smiled at them. "I was thinking," she said, "Olivia, how would you like for Poppy, KC and Sam to sleep over on Friday night? It'll be your last weekend in Lyon Place. We're packing up and moving all the furniture next week."

Olivia looked gloomy, and then brightened up. "If we have to go, I'd like that." She looked at the friends. "Is that okay?"

"Oh, yes!" said KC, answering for all three of them. "A sleepover! That's so exciting!"

Poppy, KC and Sam said goodbye to Olivia and her mum, and started to walk home. They didn't see Luke and Lucy, who had been listening from behind the hedge at the edge of the schoolyard.

When Poppy, KC and Sam were gone, Luke

and Lucy ran up to Olivia and her mum. "Hello, Olivia," said Lucy. "Sorry we were so rude yesterday. We think you're really pretty – don't we, Luke?"

Luke grunted.

"We were so stupid. Please say you forgive us," begged Lucy.

Olivia didn't know what to say. "Um, I guess."

"So, can we come to your sleepover?" Lucy asked.

"I, um . . . well . . ." Olivia didn't really want Luke and Lucy to come.

Olivia's mum interrupted. "If you're Olivia's friends, of course you can come!" she said.

"Okay, great, well, got to go, bye!" Lucy said, and the twins ran off, giggling.

"I'm very impressed with Olivia," thought her mum as they got into their car. "Making so many friends in only two days!"

"I hope those two are really okay," Olivia was thinking. "I want to make friends, but I'm really not sure about Luke and Lucy!"

Chapter 5
The Pirate Statue

All that Poppy could think about the next day at school was pirate treasure! When they were doing maths, she saw all the sums making piles of big gold coins. In music class, Poppy wanted to sing 'Yo ho ho". In art, she even made an eye-patch out of felt.

"What did pirates do?" thought Poppy. "What did they think about? If I can think like a pirate, maybe I can work out where one would hide his treasure."

By the time school was over and Poppy met up with KC and Sam, she was bursting to start looking for clues. She felt sure there would be something in the museum that would help them find the map

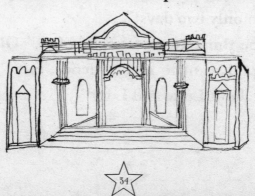

and the treasure.

"What are we waiting for?" said Poppy, slinging her backpack across her shoulders. "Let's go!"

It wasn't long before Poppy, KC and Sam were back in the museum. Poppy noticed a sign to a section about the Age of Pirates, and they ran to the display. It was a little disappointing. There was only one old cabinet with a bunch of papers in it. Poppy squinted into the case.

"None of this looks like clues," she said. "It's all just old diaries and books full of figures. I don't see what's so piratey about that."

Mr. Grant, the security guard, came around the corner. "Not impressed with our pirate memorabilia?" he asked.

"Not really," said Sam. "Pirates didn't write stuff down! They fought with swords."

"They called it swashbuckling," said Mr. Grant.

"And stole treasure," said KC.

"That was known as booty," Mr. Grant explained.

"And always had loads of gold coins," added Poppy.

"Dubloons!" said Mr. Grant. "They were the old coins pirates had. Dubloons were shiny, and each one was the size of one of your hands." Poppy remembered the big gold coins in the painting of Crossbones Charlie. Could they really still be somewhere in Lyon Place?

"I can see you're all true pirate fans," said Mr. Grant. "I don't suppose you'd be interested in seeing something a bit more . . . swashbuckling, would you? It's about Crossbones Charlie."

"Oh, yes!" said Poppy. "We'd love to!"

Mr. Grant led them down a small, tiled passage that led to the offices of the museum. Mrs. MacArthur sat behind a desk. Mr. Grant left the children at the door of the office and spoke with her. Eventually, they saw her nod her head. She got up and looked at the children over her glasses.

"I suppose, because these are the children that alerted us to the theft of the map, they may be permitted a look at the work in progress," she sniffed.

"The theft? So the map was stolen!" Poppy said.

Mrs. MacArthur looked at her disapprovingly.

"Indeed it was," she said. "It's really quite a mystery. I was very angry with Mr. Grant for letting it happen." Mr. Grant looked very upset.

"If only we'd got there just a little bit earlier," thought Poppy, "We might have seen who took the map."

Mrs. MacArthur told them to follow her, and opened a small door in the office. The friends thought it might lead to a broom cupboard or a kitchen, but it opened into a wide room, filled with ancient-looking things. In one corner, a skeleton of something with two legs and a long neck seemed to peer over at them. Swords lay on a wooden rack. A stuffed crocodile hung from the ceiling.

"This," said Mrs. MacArthur, sounding proud, "is where our Work In Progress is kept."

"That's everything the museum works on, before it's put on exhibition," explained Mr. Grant. "Like that ostrich skeleton over there. It's still missing some bones that need to be put back on."

"It's an ostrich?" asked KC. "I thought it was a dinosaur!"

"You'll be surprised how different things can be when you take a second look," said Mr. Grant. "And talking of looking, take a peek at Crossbones Charlie himself!"

He threw back a sheet that was covering something tall, and the children saw a large wooden statue. It was a statue of a man in a three-cornered hat, holding a sword and a flag that fell across his jacket in wooden folds. The wood was nearly black with age, and there were small holes through the bottom of the statue, but it still looked almost alive. The face had that same fierce grin that the painting had in Lyon Place. It was Crossbones Charlie again!

"We're restoring him. He'll be back on display in the museum soon," said Mrs. MacArthur. "Of course, Charlie Lyon had this statue made of himself. It used to sit on the staircase at Lyon Place, until it was given to us by the Lyon Family many years ago. They said," she sniffed, "it gave them the creeps."

Poppy didn't think the statue looked creepy at all. She reached out to stroke the wood.

"Don't touch!" cried Mrs. MacArthur. "It's very delicate."

Poppy drew back her hand and looked at the wooden flag Charlie was holding. It had a curious design on it. There was a diagonal cross, and at each corner of the cross was a rectangle shape.

Poppy pointed to it. "Why does Charlie's flag look like that?"

Mrs. MacArthur peered at it. "I don't know. Charlie Lyon was famous for his skull and crossbones flag. That's why they called him Crossbones Charlie. But this looks different." She clapped her hands. "I must get back to work, and so must you, Mr. Grant. No more maps going missing!"

Poppy, KC and Sam sat on the steps of the museum, trying their hardest to think what to do next.

"It was cool to see the statue," said KC, trying to put a brave face on things, as always.

"I guess so," Sam said. "Those marks on Charlie's flag were strange. I'm sure they must be a clue. But nothing we saw helped us find the map."

Poppy was thinking. "I keep thinking of something Mr. Grant said, but I'm not sure why. Something about looking twice . . . I know!" Poppy sprang up. "He said, 'you'll be surprised how different things can be when you take a second look'!"

"So what?" said Sam.

"I've just realised that we had a clue on us all the time, and we never looked at it again," said Poppy, feeling in her backpack. "The pieces of paper that led us to the missing map!"

She took them out and showed them to KC and Sam. They were three small pieces of paper. For the first time, they bent over them, took one each, and looked hard.

Sam held his piece up to the light. "They're ripped from a bigger piece of paper. Maybe all the same one," he said. "That could be important."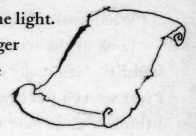

KC turned hers over. "Look! There are some words on the back! I can just about see them. They look strange."

Poppy looked at her piece, the one that said 'THE MAP IS ON THE WALL IN THE NEXT ROOM. YOU DON'T HAVE MUCH TIME!'

"It's strange," she said. "I never really thought about who left these clues. I just thought they were, well, clues. But what if these pieces of paper were for someone else? What ..." Poppy said, thinking out loud, "... what if they were for the thief?"

"But why would a thief need clues to steal a painting? And who'd leave them?" asked Sam.

"I don't know," said Poppy. "It's just a hunch!"

KC had been rummaging around in her bag. "I know it's in here somewhere ..." she said. She held something from her bag up to the paper, and peered at it. "Awesome! It works!" she beamed.

"What works?" asked Sam.

"Look at the writing on the back of the note," said KC. "It's really faint, but you can just see it. I just worked out that the writing was backwards. I think it must have been from another page that was put down on top of it when the ink wasn't dry, so it left a mark."

"Nice work, KC," said Poppy. "That's good detecting."

KC looked pleased. "That's not all, though," she said. "I've got a mirror in my bag – my little purple mirror on my hairbrush – and I looked at the words in the mirror. It reverses them, so you can read them!"

Sam and Poppy looked admiringly at KC, who smiled. "I guess today was my lucky day."

"Not your lucky day – your VERY CLEVER day!" said Poppy. "So, what does it say?"

KC held the little mirror up to the note again. "It's an address! 223 Main Street. That's in the centre of town, not far away."

Poppy put her backpack on her shoulder. "Then let's go see!"

Chapter 6
The Man with the Map

Poppy, KC and Sam walked through town. Most of the stores were starting to close, and people were on bikes, in cars and on foot. Poppy tried to remember the shops on Main Street. There was the Post Office, the grocery store, the bakery. She didn't think it could be any of those. Only a few stores had numbers on them, so the friends had to count down to 223. When they reached it, they saw that it was a store with a big glass window full of brass knick-knacks, books and old furniture. The words 'CAXTON'S ANTIQUES' were written in a wide curve at the top of the window.

"This must be it," said Sam.

As he spoke, a man in a brown jacket came to the window from inside the store and pulled down a wide blind. They couldn't see anything in the store any more.

KC sighed. "I guess we got here too late," she said. "Let's come back tomorrow. Maybe that man knows something about the missing map."

"Wait," said Poppy, her green eyes narrowing as she thought quickly. "Let's go around back. Maybe we can see inside."

Sam and KC looked doubtful. "I don't know, Poppy," said Sam. "What if someone sees us?"

But Poppy was already running off down the narrow lane between the shops. "They won't!" she said, confidently. There was nothing else for KC and Sam to do but to follow her.

Behind the store, things looked very different. Unlike the cheerful, busy front, everything was grey and deserted. The antique store was part of a group of buildings on Main Street, huddled next to each other. A couple of small windows peered out of grimy red brick. A black fire escape hung on the wall next to a battered door with peeling green paint. There wasn't anyone around.

Poppy walked up to two metal trash cans that stood near the windows. She pointed to them, and made an upwards gesture. KC and Sam looked at each other, and nodded. Poppy was already trying to scramble onto one of them, and they helped her up.

"What can you see?" hissed KC. "Is there anybody there?"

Poppy could see through the window into a tiny back office, lit by a single lamp. As she watched, the man in the brown jacket entered the room. He glanced around and opened a filing cabinet. Poppy held her breath as he pulled a large cardboard tube out of the cabinet, and drew something out of the tube. He carefully smoothed it onto the table.

It was a large square piece of parchment. In the dim light Poppy could see that the lines on it marked out the place of rooms and floors on a house.

"A map!" she whispered to the others. "He's got a map."

The man touched the paper gently, and said something to himself that Poppy couldn't hear. Poppy leaned over to try and see the map better. There were some large letters in one corner. As the man moved his hand, Poppy strained her eyes to read them.

"LYON PLACE!" she said, in a kind of whispering shout. She looked down at the others, wide-eyed as they stared at her. "It's the missing map!"

Sam wanted to climb up to see, but Poppy motioned to him to be still. The man pulled out another piece of paper. This one was clean and new, with a different floor plan. He nodded to himself, and put the new piece of paper back again. Then he rolled the map back up into the big cardboard tube.

But instead of putting the tube back in the cabinet, he tucked it under his arm, got up and switched the light off. He walked back through the doorway to the main part of the shop. Poppy scrambled off the trash can as quickly and quietly as she could.

"Is he coming out this way?" asked KC, looking ready to run.

"No," whispered Poppy. "He's going out the front. With the map! We have to follow him."

The three friends dashed out from the back of the store. They peered around the corner, and saw the man in the brown jacket come out of the front of the shop and lock it up. He was carrying a briefcase as well as the cardboard tube. He put on an old-fashioned grey felt hat, and set off down the street. In a few moments, he was out of sight among the throngs of people.

"We can't lose him," said Poppy. "If we lose him, we lose the map . . . and the treasure!"

Poppy, KC and Sam tried to thread their way through the crowd. Suddenly, people seemed to be everywhere. KC almost bumped into a small child. Sam had to duck between a couple holding hands. Poppy stuck close to the wall, and caught a glimpse of the grey felt hat turning a corner.

"I see him!" she called, and Sam and KC ran to her. Poppy weaved through the crowd to reach the corner. There were far less people on the next street. Poppy was relieved to see the man in the brown jacket heading away from the crowds.

"We can't get too close," said Poppy, "Or he'll spot us. We have to hang back."

"If we hang too far back, we'll lose him!" said Sam.

"He's getting away again!" KC said, and they set off down the street.

It was hard work, keeping the brown jacket in view but keeping themselves out of sight. The man didn't seem to be in a hurry. He walked into the park, and the friends followed him. Just inside the gates, he stopped. He yawned, stretched, and . . . turned around! Poppy, KC and Sam stood rooted to the spot. They didn't know what to do!

Chapter 7

The Map Comes Back

The man in the brown jacket looked around the park, still holding the cardboard tube under his arm. His gaze fell on the three friends, and then moved on. Poppy felt she could breathe again.

"He doesn't know we've been following him!" she said. "He thinks we're just three kids. Don't look at him!"

"What do we do?" asked KC. "Do we pretend to talk to each other?"

"We are talking to each other," Sam reminded her.

"Oh, yes," said KC lamely. "But I'll bet we look really guilty!"

Poppy risked taking a look at the man. He yawned and walked on a little way, then sat on a park bench. He patted the cardboard tube, and then took out a newspaper from his briefcase.

"What's he doing now?" asked Sam, exasperated. "He can't just start reading when he's carrying the missing map!"

"Shh," said Poppy. "We have to wait for his next move. Let's try to get a bit closer to him!"

As the man continued to read the newspaper, the three friends crept into the undergrowth behind him. It was difficult not to make noise, but if they stared through the bushes, they could see the man, contentedly leafing through the news.

Sam had an idea. "If I can just get a bit closer," he said, "I think I can grab the map." He started to inch forward.

"No, Sam!" hissed Poppy, grabbing his arm. "It's too dangerous! We have to see where he takes it!"

"Maybe he's going to sell it," said KC, as quietly as she could. "If it says where Crossbones Charlie's treasure is, maybe someone could buy it, get the treasure and be rich!"

"Maybe he'll throw it away, and we can pick it up!" said Poppy, hopefully. She stuck her head out of the bush. The man looked calmly around, and she quickly stuck it back in again. "That was close!"

"Whatever," said Sam. "I think he's going to burn it or rip it to pieces. And then we'll never get the treasure!"

"I don't mind what he does," whispered KC, "As long as he does something. There's a spider over here in the bush, and he keeps looking at me in a funny way!"

The man didn't pass the map to anyone else, or burn it, or throw it away. Instead, he stretched and put his paper back in his briefcase. Then he got up and started walking away again.

"Back to following him!" said Poppy, and they crept back out of the bushes.

Now the friends knew they had to be extra careful. The man had seen all three of them. If he noticed them again, he might realise that he was being followed. Poppy, KC and Sam kept behind trees in the park, only running out once the man had turned a corner and gone back out of the park.

"I hope he gets where he's going soon," said Sam. "My feet are getting tired of sneaking around."

The friends tracked him along a few more streets, until the man was standing outside the museum. He paused, then went inside. The friends waited until he had entered, and then scrambled up the wide entrance steps.

"What is he doing?" wondered KC. "Why is he going back in there?"

But all Poppy could do was shake her head in confusion.

From around a corner, they watched as the man headed down the same narrow corridor they'd taken earlier. "He's going to Mrs. MacArthur's office," Sam said. "I don't understand!"

"Nor do I," said KC

They waited and waited outside the office for the man to come out again. Poppy wondered if the man had found a way out of the other door in the office.

Suddenly, the door was thrown open and the man came out. Mrs. MacArthur was with him.

"Thank you so much, Mr. Caxton," she said. "The museum and I owe you an incalculable debt!"

"Not at all, not at all," said the man. "Anything to be of service to this venerable institution."

"What do those words mean?" asked Sam.

"And what are they talking about?" asked KC.

"I don't know!" answered Poppy. She hated not knowing.

As Mr. Caxton put on his hat and turned to go, he caught sight of the three friends. Just like in the park, they found it was too late to move. They could only stare guiltily at him.

He looked at them suspiciously. "Haven't I seen you three before?"

Poppy, KC and Sam shook their heads silently. Poppy noticed that he wasn't carrying the map any more.

Mr. Caxton gave them another long look, shrugged and walked off. The friends rushed into the office, all trying to speak at once.

"He had the map!"

"We followed him!"

"It's in the tube!"

Mrs. MacArthur was sitting back at her desk. She looked up, annoyed. "What? Why are you children barging in here?"

Poppy was the first to reply. "Mrs. MacArthur – that man, Mr. Caxton, he had the map in a cardboard tube! He had it in his antique shop!"

Mrs. MacArthur looked at Poppy over her glasses. "I know," she said. She reached under the desk, and put a cardboard tube on top of it.

The friends gasped. Finally, the missing map was nearly in their grasp!

Mrs. MacArthur's bony hand descended on the tube and held it. "Mr. Caxton found the map posted through his letterbox this morning," she said. "He realised it must belong to the museum, so he returned it. That is all."

"But –" Poppy didn't know what to say. "The man – Mr. Caxton – we found his address from the clues on the floor –"

Mrs. MacArthur pursed her lips. "That's enough, young lady," she said. "I haven't got time to listen to your stories right now."

"Can we just have a look at the map?" KC asked in a trembling voice. She already knew what Mrs. MacArthur would say.

"Certainly not. The map is in a very delicate state. And it must be checked for fingerprints. Mr. Caxton specifically told me that nobody should touch it until it's back on the wall where it belongs. You may see it there, and not before." She put the tube with the map in behind the desk, and glared at them. "And now, would you kindly leave the office!"

There was nothing for it but to head home again. It was so annoying.

Chapter 8
Secrets at the Sleepover

Poppy and Sam were gloomy as they walked to Lyon Place the next day. Even the prospect of a night at the big old house didn't cheer them up much. It was the evening of the sleepover, and that meant it was the last weekend Olivia would ever spend in Lyon Place.

"Just think," said Poppy. "The missing map is back in the museum, and we didn't even get to see it!"

The two of them had been talking about Mr. Caxton and his strange behaviour as they walked.

"Mr. Caxton does have something to do with the map," Poppy said. "Otherwise, why would his address have been on the clues? If Mrs. MacArthur had listened to us, we could have explained."

"Whatever," said Sam, gloomily. "Unless we can find the treasure tonight, Lyon Place is gone. We have to find it tonight!"

They knocked on the old brass doorknocker and

Olivia let them in. KC was already waiting behind her.

"Hi," said Olivia. "We're going to have a great time!" But Poppy and Sam could see that her eyes were red, as if she'd been crying.

Poppy whispered in her ear. "It's okay, Olivia. When everyone else is asleep tonight, we'll look all through the house for one last time. Who knows, we might find the treasure!"

Olivia brightened up a little and squeezed Poppy's arm as if to thank her.

Olivia's mother appeared at the top of the steps down to the kitchen, holding a big tray full of food and drinks. "Good evening, everyone. Would anyone like some lemonade?"

The friends all went into the family room to eat.

Poppy looked up at the high ceilings and the shadowy corners. Although there was a big TV and comfy looking sofas, they sat in the middle of the room, far from the walls.

"I've never seen such a big room," she said.

Olivia's mum smiled. "Far too big for us, really! It's probably a good thing we'll be moving somewhere more cosy."

But Poppy could see that she didn't look very happy, either. For a moment, Poppy thought about telling her about their plan to find the treasure tonight. But then she decided to keep quiet. Grown-ups didn't always understand about detecting.

Olivia's mum put the tray down. It was filled with vegetables and dips and thick pizza slices, glasses of lemonade and flapjacks. Poppy saw Sam's eyes widen as he licked his lips.

"I hope you enjoy it," said Olivia's mum as she left. "I'm sorry it's not home-made food, but we've already had the fridge taken away. I'll be in the kitchen if you need me."

Just as Sam was just about to bite into his first slice of pizza, they heard a knocking at the door. Several hard, fast knocks, as if the knocker wanted very much to get in. They heard Olivia's mum open the door and say hello.

And then before they knew it, Luke and Lucy were striding into the room!

Olivia looked nervous. "Oh, I forgot to tell you, Poppy," Olivia said nervously. "Luke and Lucy said they were sorry for being rude, so I, er, invited them over tonight!"

Luke and Lucy were holding big sleeping bags. They looked at Poppy, Sam, KC and Olivia with nasty smiles.

Poppy stood up. "You two had better not cause any trouble!"

"Too late now," said Luke. "We're here, anyway." He picked up two slices of pizza, pressed them together, and pushed them into his mouth.

Lucy sat down on the sofa, pushing Olivia and Poppy out of the way. "We're here to hunt for treasure," she said. "And we're not going away, so you'd better get used to it!"

"I'm sorry, Poppy," said Olivia. "I thought they'd changed."

Poppy smiled sadly at Olivia. "Those two never

change!"

The four friends realised that they were in for a difficult night. Luke ate so fast that there was hardly any food left for anyone else. Lucy kept pushing everyone out of the way and talking loudly about what she was going to buy when she found the treasure.

Everyone watched a DVD when they had finished eating, but Lucy wouldn't stop talking, so it was hard to hear what was happening. And Luke sat right in front of the TV, so it was hard to see, too.

By the time they were all ready for bed, Poppy was furious with the two uninvited guests. She beckoned to KC and Olivia, and told Olivia all about how they'd followed Mr. Caxton, and how the map had been returned. "But we don't need the map," said Poppy hopefully. "When they've gone to bed, we'll go around the house and try to find the treasure."

But sneaky Lucy had overheard them. "Don't bother trying to look for the treasure without us," she said. "We're not going to go to sleep until we've found it. And then I can buy anything I want!"

Olivia's mum came in to make sure they were all in their sleeping bags. She kissed Olivia good night (which made Lucy snort) and then went upstairs. Soon, all the lights were turned low and the house was quiet. Olivia's mum would have been surprised to see all the children get out of their sleeping bags, as quietly as they could, and get ready to explore.

Sam had bought his small torch, which was built into the top of a pen. KC had a big torch she'd borrowed from home. Its beam seemed to sweep the darkness away and make everything a lot less creepy.

"You're not scared of the dark, are you?" Lucy asked KC.

KC shivered. "Maybe just a little," she said, and huddled closer to Poppy.

"What a baby," said Lucy. "We don't need torches do we, Luke?"

Luke didn't look so sure. "Um, I guess not," he mumbled, and stood closer to his twin.

Chapter 9

Explorers

Poppy led the expedition around Lyon Place in the dark.

They started with the room they were in. Everyone shone torches, looking for signs of a hidden panel. Sam peered up at paintings to see if there were any secret latches or locks. But there was nothing.

"I've looked in this room a thousand times," sighed Olivia. "Let's try the hall."

It was annoying to have Luke and Lucy there. But, with so many people, Poppy felt braver.

She opened the door and they all crept out. With a few hall lights glowing softly, they only used the torches to light where they were looking.

After a few minutes, Luke yawned. "I'm bored. Let's look somewhere else!"

"We're not finished here yet," Poppy hissed. "If you're bored, get back in your sleeping bag!"

That made Luke keep quiet. KC gave Poppy the

thumbs-up, and Poppy grinned back at her.

The team went from room to room, searching downstairs. But they didn't find even a single thing.

"Okay," said Poppy. "Only one more room to go down here, then –" She felt someone take KC's torch out of her hands. "Hey!"

Lucy waved the torch, laughing softly. "We're going to look upstairs! You can stay down here if you like." She started climbing the staircase, with Luke following.

"No, wait!" Olivia called, as loudly as she dared. But it was too late. Lucy and Luke were already upstairs, making far too much noise.

"We can't go up there yet," explained Olivia, "because my mum will still be awake." Just then, the friends heard the sound of a door opening.

Luke and Lucy came hurtling downstairs, straight into the family room.

"Hello?" Olivia's mum called from upstairs. "Is that you, children? I thought I heard a noise." A light went on upstairs and the friends quickly followed Luke and Lucy. Inside, Luke and Lucy were already burrowing into their sleeping bags. As Olivia's mum came downstairs, Sam switched off his pen-torch and they all dived inside the sleeping bags.

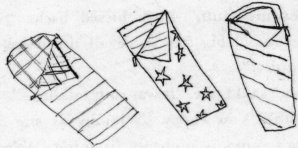

"Ow!" said Lucy. "KC, stop trying to climb in my bag!"

"Oh, sorry," said KC, "I thought it was mine." She scrambled into the last empty sleeping bag, one second before Olivia's mum came and turned the lights on.

All she saw was a room full of sleeping children. Some of them were even making loud snoring sounds.

"Well," she said, "since you're all asleep, I guess none of you can hear me. So there's no point in saying that if I hear any more sounds, there'll be trouble!" She smiled to herself, turned out the light, and left the room.

Nobody spoke for ages. Eventually, Olivia dared to whisper. "Oh, nice work, Lucy! Now we'll never be able to go upstairs and explore."

"Not my fault," Lucy hissed back. "Stupid Luke's stupid big feet made all the noise. He's never quiet!"

"Hey," said Luke, "It was your talking –"

"Shhh!" said Poppy, as loudly as she dared. "Olivia's mum is probably listening. We're just going to have to stop exploring and go to sleep."

Everyone groaned quietly. But with Olivia's mum on the lookout, it was the only thing to do.

Light on Poppy's eyelids made her wake up. She looked around to find everyone else sleeping. Luke was snoring for real this time.

"It must be very early morning," Poppy thought. She was very thirsty. Luke had drunk most of the lemonade last night. She tried to get back to sleep, but soon realised it was useless. She needed a drink.

Quietly, Poppy got out of her sleeping bag and stepped over the others to get to the door. Turning the handle noiselessly, she padded across the hall and over to the big steps leading down to the kitchen. They were cold on her bare feet. Poppy just wanted to get some water, and go back to sleep.

She'd forgotten how big the kitchen was. It looked bare and empty in the bleak early morning light. Most of the appliances were already gone from the room, but she remembered how warm and welcoming it had been the last time she'd visited. "I hope the people who live here next will make it nice again," she thought.

Poppy took a clean glass from the rack by the sink, and started to fill it with water. She shivered suddenly. There was a tiny, cold breeze around her feet. She looked around, but she couldn't see an open window anywhere.

"There must be a hole, or a gap, or something," Poppy thought. She went to the back door, but it wasn't coming from there. It seemed to be coming from the wall where the fridge had been.

Poppy crouched down by the wall. Right at the bottom, almost hidden by dust and fluff, a thin tear in the flowery wallpaper was letting the cold in.

Poppy stood up, suddenly awake. Gently, she knocked on the wall. Instead of the dull thump she was expecting, she heard a hollow sound. A sound with the tiniest echo. Cautiously, she knocked a little harder. The whole section of wall moved a bit. Just the tiniest fraction. But it was enough for Poppy to see that it had creased the wallpaper around it. In the shape of a door! Olivia's parents must have been too busy packing to notice it!

Poppy gasped and gave the wall another push. The wallpaper tore a little, with a ripping sound that seemed loud enough to wake the house.

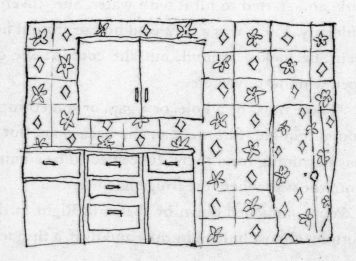

A couple more pushes, and the paper around the door was almost free from the wall. Poppy gave the wall a final shove ... and a door opened away from her with a creak.

All Poppy could see was darkness, stretching in front of her.

Chapter 10

Into the Dark

KC wriggled. Something was tickling her ear. She woke up to find Poppy's face next to hers. Poppy looked excited, anxious, scared and happy all at once.

"KC! Wake up! I've found it! I've really found a secret passage!" Poppy whispered fiercely.

KC squinted, yawned and rubbed her eyes. She looked at Poppy in amazement. "How —"

Poppy put her finger to her lips. "Quiet! We don't want to wake Luke and Lucy. They'll ruin it all again, just like last night!"

KC stood up as quietly as she could. Poppy grabbed KC's big flashlight and tiptoed over to Sam's sleeping bag. He was fast asleep. Poppy touched his shoulder, and he turned over. "High score . . ." he muttered in his sleep. "Level ten . . ."

"He's dreaming about videogames," Poppy whispered. She prodded Sam in the shoulder. He batted her hand away and pulled the pillow over his head. "Whatever," he said sleepily.

Poppy shook Sam's shoulder. He woke with a start.

Poppy clamped a hand over his mouth. Behind him, Luke and Lucy both stirred. They were on either side of Olivia, who was still asleep. Poppy held Sam until they had stopped moving again, then whispered about the door. His eyes widened, and he jumped out of the sleeping bag.

"We can't wake Olivia," she whispered, "Or they'll wake up, too. Come on!" They put on their slippers and left the room, trying not to make any noise.

Poppy didn't say anything else until they were in the kitchen, gazing at the dark opening. KC shuddered a little as she looked down into it.

"It's the cellars," said Sam, nodding.

"How do you know?" asked Poppy.

"I read it on the computer," explained Sam. "It said Lyon House had cellars for wine and coal and stuff. You know, in the old days. I didn't know they were still there."

Poppy shone KC's flashlight into the dark. It

showed a set of stone steps leading down. KC looked worried, and Sam looked excited. They knew what she wanted to do.

"This could be our biggest adventure yet," Poppy whispered. "I'll go first!"

Poppy took the first steps down the staircase. The air was cold and smelled dry and dusty. Poppy shone KC's flashlight in front of her to see where she was going. Behind her, she heard Sam and KC.

"Sam," said KC, "could I hold your pen-torch?"

"Sure," said Sam, and passed it to her. Poppy and Sam knew that KC didn't like the dark very much.

Poppy stepped off the last stair and swung the torch around. A long passage stretched in front of her. On both sides, tall shelves lined the walls. Most of the shelves were empty, but one or two had old bottles still stacked on them. KC and Sam joined her. "I wish we had Millie with us," said KC. "Cats can see in the dark."

"This must have been where they kept the wine," said Sam. His voice echoed down the corridor.

"What do you think is down there?"

"Treasure," said Poppy firmly. The friends felt a wave of excitement rush through them. They had found a real hidden passage. It had to be where the treasure was hidden.

They walked slowly along the arched passage, shining the torches on every surface. Soon, they could see that the passageway split into two, both ways leading into more darkness.

"You know what we should do?" said Poppy. "We should split up."

"Oh, no, Poppy, no way!" squealed KC. "We've got to —" she shone her torch onto Poppy's face and saw her smile.

"Only joking, KC!" said Poppy. "Don't worry. We won't lose you. We're going to explore this place together!"

They took the passage on the right and crept cautiously along. Sam touched the wall and looked at his fingers. "Look!" he said. "The walls have turned my fingers black."

"This must be where they kept the coal," said Poppy. "They would take it up in bits to burn in the fireplaces. It's how they kept Lyon Place warm." Poppy coughed. Their feet were stirring up the coal dust, and everything seemed even blacker than before. "I don't think we should go much further this way," said Poppy. "If I were a pirate, I wouldn't bury my treasure in coal." Sam and KC agreed, and they turned back to take the other path.

KC paused as they passed the junction again. "Did you hear that?"

Poppy stopped and listened. "No, I didn't hear anything. Come on."

But KC stood still for a second or two. "I thought I heard a sound."

 "Probably mice," said Sam. "You always get mice in these places."

"How do you know?" asked Poppy. "You've never been in a secret passage before!"

"Whatever," said Sam. "I just know. I've read loads of stories with secret passages in them."

"Mice are fine," said KC. "I'm not scared of mice. My cousin used to have a pet –"

A swinging, slamming kind of sound crashed

through the darkness. The three friends jumped.

KC was the first to speak. "I told you so," she said. "Someone's down here!" She began to walk more quickly, and Poppy and Sam had to trot to keep pace with her. They reached another split in the passage. This time, it was a crossroads, with three ways to choose from. They looked down all three, but couldn't hear anything, or see anyone.

"I'm sure it was just the door closing behind us," said Poppy. Then she wished she hadn't said it. KC looked very scared.

"I don't like this any more – Poppy – I don't like it! We should come back with some grown ups and –"

KC stopped and listened. There was no mistaking the sound this time. It was a spooky wail, and it seemed to be coming from everywhere!

KC shrieked and ran, knocking the torch out of Poppy's hand. By the time Poppy had picked it up and shone it anxiously round the crossroads, KC was nowhere to be seen. She pointed the torch at Sam. "We have to find her," she said.

Sam gulped and nodded. "What was that

sound?"

Poppy looked grimly into the dark. "I've got a sneaky suspicion that we're not the only ones down here. Let's try this way. I'm pretty sure KC went down here."

"What do you mean?" asked Sam nervously. "You mean there might be . . . ghosts?"

Poppy shook her head. "No. I mean, I think Luke and Lucy might have found our secret passage, too!"

KC kept running for a while, the thin light of the pen-torch flickering in front of her. She stopped and caught her breath. How silly she'd been! She knew she was safe with Poppy and Sam. After all, she told herself, they were still in good old Lyon Place. Just . . . under it. She flashed the torch behind her, but could see only dusty brick walls.

KC was scared of the dark. But it wasn't the dark that really scared her. It was what her imagination put into it! She was very glad of the pen-torch.

"I'll just turn around and go back to the crossroads," KC thought to herself. "Poppy must think I'm a scaredy-cat. But I really did hear a sound!"

KC turned around and started to make her way back the way she came. "Poppy?" she called, listening to the echoes of her voice. She was very relieved to hear Poppy and Sam calling to her. They didn't sound too far off.

And then another sound made KC jump. It was the same wailing sound as before. "Wooooooh!" it went. "Wooooooh!"

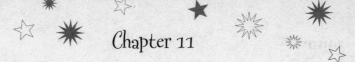

Chapter 11

Voices Underground

KC stopped and tried to stay calm. "He-hello?" she called.

"Wooooh!" came the voice again. "This is the voice of Charlie!"

"Charlie?" KC said into the darkness. "Charlie who?"

"WOOOOH! Lazybones Charlie, the Pirate!"

KC was puzzled as well as scared. "Do you mean Crossbones Charlie?"

"Woooh! Yes! That one! Crossbones Charlie! KC, I will never let you out of here unless you tell me one thing! If you answer falsely, you will have to stay down here for all eternity!"

KC listened to the voice. Now that she thought about it, it sounded awfully familiar for a ghost pirate. "What kind of ghost doesn't know its own name?" she thought.

"KC! You must tell us what your name is! Your full name! What does KC stand for?"

KC wasn't frightened any more. She realised what must have happened. Luke and Lucy must have woken up and found the open door in the kitchen, and then come down to scare them!

"I'm no scaredy-cat," she thought. "I'll show them!"

She made her voice sound quavery and scared. "Oh, great ghost pirate!" she called out. "Why don't I tell you where your treasure is hidden, instead?"

There was a pause. KC thought she could hear Luke and Lucy arguing. Lucy called out again in her ghost pirate voice. "Yes . . . yes, that would be even better. Quick, KC, tell me where the treasure is . . . and we will spare you!"

"We?" shouted KC. "Don't you mean 'I'?"

"Oh, yes, 'I'! WOOOOOH!"

KC gave them some directions and heard two sets of feet scamper off, away from her. She giggled. If only Poppy and Sam had been here to hear that! Now that Luke and Lucy were gone, KC suddenly found she didn't feel scared anymore. "After all," she told herself, "I've just tricked two annoying 'ghosts', all on my own!"

KC set off back down the passage again, and soon reached the crossroads. Shining her torch all around, she saw two anxious faces appear down one of the passageways. Poppy and Sam! She ran to them and told them what had happened, and they laughed with her. Even the spooky echoes of the laughter couldn't stop KC feeling glad she'd been so brave.

The friends walked up the right-hand passage from the crossroads. The corridor seemed to go on forever. They began to shiver.

"It's cold down here," said Sam. "I wish we'd brought coats."

Poppy tracked the beam of her torch over the bricks. She stopped. "Look!" she said. "There's a gap in the bricks!"

They knelt down to look at it. Sure enough, there was a small hole at the bottom of the wall, where some bricks had tumbled over. Poppy shone KC's torch through it. "That's strange," she said. I can see stairs leading up!"

Sam looked through the hole. "I think we should carry on. Who knows what's up there?"

"I think we should investigate," said Poppy. "KC, what do you think?"

Half an hour ago, KC would have thought that there was no way she would go through a hole like that. But now she felt much braver. She squeezed Poppy's hand. "Let's go through!"

They looked at Sam, who shrugged. "You're both crazy," he said. But he followed them into the hole.

On the other side, they found they could stand up again. The stairs rose up in front of them, surrounded by junk. Unlike the stone stairs that went into the cellars, these stairs were made of wood. They looked old and almost rotten. When Poppy put her foot on the first one, it creaked loudly.

She took the next step carefully and shone the torch upwards. "I can see a door," she said. "It's a way out!" She climbed a few more steps, and they creaked and squealed underneath her.

KC went up next, with Sam coming last. They moved as slowly as they could.

"What if the steps break?" asked KC quietly.

"Oh, don't worry about that," said Sam, cheerfully, from behind her. "It would be much worse if the whole staircase was rotten and it started to fall – aah!" They heard a sharp crack.

Poppy and KC stopped and turned around in fright. Sam was clambering up to the next step, looking pale. "The step broke," he said. "I got onto the next one okay, though. I'm fine!"

Sam didn't say anything else on the way up. And he tested every step very carefully, too.

Poppy tried the door at the top of the stairs. It opened just enough for her to squeeze through.

"What's up there, Poppy?" called KC.

"Lots more junk, I think," said Poppy. "Come on up and see! It's pretty dark, though. I can hardly see anything."

KC and Sam squeezed through the gap, into a big room. A couple of high windows let some early morning light in, but it was hard to see clearly. Strange shapes loomed everywhere.

Suddenly, lights flickered on all over the room. After so much gloom, the friends couldn't see anything for a second or two.

"Who's there? Show yourselves!"

The grown up voice was loud and stern. The friends could now make out a figure in a peaked blue cap heading towards them. "I know you're here," it said. "Come out!"

Poppy was the first to recognise him. "Mr. Grant! It's us – Poppy, KC and Sam!"

Mr. Grant took off his cap and scratched his head in puzzlement. "You three? But how did you get in the museum? You don't mean to say you've been here all night?"

"We're in the museum?" said KC. "I don't believe it!"

"Mr. Grant – we came through an underground tunnel," said Poppy. "It must go from Lyon Place to the museum!" She looked around and realised they were in the museum's workshop. The swords glinted on the rack, the statue of Crossbones Charlie sat under its canvas cover, and the ostrich skeleton rose above them.

Mr. Grant started to laugh. "Well, of all the things! We always thought that door just led down to the old storeroom. Never knew there was a way to Lyon Place down there. Seems like you've discovered a genuine secret passage!"

"Mr. Grant," said Poppy, thinking quickly, "do you believe that Crossbones Charlie's treasure is real?"

"Well," said the security guard, "If old Crossbones Charlie had a secret passage from the house to the museum, who knows?"

"In that case," said Poppy, "can we ask you for a favour?"

Minutes later, Mr. Grant was taking the map of Lyon Place off the wall. "Let's make this quick!" he told them.

Poppy looked at the map up close for the first time. It showed all the rooms on both floors of Lyon Place, as well as a small drawing of the house in one corner. There didn't seem to be anything special about it at all.

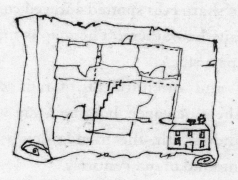

"Seems a funny thing to steal," said Mr. Grant. "Most people would just take a photograph of it, if they wanted to see it up close."

"Unless . . ." said Poppy, suddenly realising something, "The paper itself is special! That's it! That's got to be it! Mr. Grant, please, please can you take the map out of the frame?"

Mr. Grant frowned, but he loosened the back of the frame and took the map out, very carefully. "I can't let you touch this," he said. "It's just too old and delicate."

He turned the map over to show the empty back.

"Looks like the paper's just normal. Pretty thick, but that was how they made it a long time ago."

Poppy's sharp eyes spotted a frayed corner of the map. "Wait! Look there! The map is made of two pieces of paper!"

Slowly and carefully, Mr. Grant drew back the top sheet of paper. It came away with a soft rustle. Underneath, the friends saw a new map. A different kind of map entirely.

"It's a map of the cellars!" said Sam. "Look, there's where we came down – there's the crossroads, and the coal cellar."

KC pointed to a passage that was drawn with dotted lines in the faded brown ink. "And there's the secret passage that leads to the museum."

Poppy's green eyes shone as she pointed to another area on the map. "And look there."

They all followed her finger, down from the

crossroads, away from where they had explored —
to where a big X sat in bright red ink.

"Crossbones Charlie's treasure!" they all said
together. Even Mr. Grant!

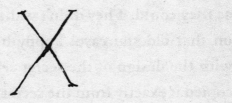

Chapter 12

Mr. Grant Saves the Day

Poppy, KC and Sam ran back to Lyon Place as fast as they could. They didn't want to take any chances on that old staircase! Poppy held a piece of paper with the design of the secret cellar map on it; she'd copied it exactly from the secret map, and Mr. Grant had put the map back on the wall.

As they rushed, panting, up to the garden of Lyon Place, they saw Olivia and her mum standing outside. They were with a stranger. Luke and Lucy were nowhere to be seen. Olivia looked sad, and her mum looked worried.

"Where have you been?" Olivia's mum asked them. "Olivia's been terribly worried about you all!"

Poppy tried to explain what had happened, but Olivia's mum interrupted. "It wasn't fair to run off like that. What if you'd gone missing?"

"But we didn't leave the house!" KC tried to explain. "That is – we did, but we didn't know we were . . . and then we came right back —"

Poppy interrupted. "We've found the treasure! We have to go inside!"

Olivia's mum handed some keys to the stranger, who looked at them sternly. "I'm Olivia's dad," he said. "I think it's best if you go home now. Fortunately, we didn't have time to call your parents, so they won't know how worried we've been."

"But, really, we have to go inside," said Poppy. "Into the cellars. There's a secret passage! Olivia, don't you believe me?"

But Olivia just looked at them with a bad-tempered expression. "I woke up, and you were all gone," she said. "Even Luke and Lucy! They came back and they were covered in soot! They said you all went down to the cellars, and then you ran off outside. Luke and Lucy said they tried to stop you, but you wouldn't wait. Why didn't you wake me up? It's not fair!"

This wasn't what the friends were expecting. They had thought that they could go inside and find the treasure right away. "But —" said Poppy again.

"But nothing," said Olivia's dad. "Those cellars have been closed for years, and for a good reason. They're too dangerous to play in. Now, please. Off you go." He handed them their bags.

Poppy tried to meet Olivia's eye, but she hung on to her mum and didn't look back at Poppy. There was nothing else to do but go.

They walked slowly back along the wide street. "What's the good of knowing where the treasure is, if nobody believes us?" said Sam.

"And we can't get Mr. Grant to tell them, either. We promised not to tell anyone he helped us," KC reminded them.

The only fun part of their walk was when Luke and Lucy emerged from the shelter of a nearby bush. They were both covered in coal dust. Luke was coughing, and Lucy was trying frantically to brush it out of her hair. "You!" she pointed at KC. "There's no treasure in that stupid cellar. We looked through the coal for AGES!"

The friends had to laugh. "I didn't tell you anything," KC said. "I only spoke to the ghost of Crossbones Charlie!"

"WOOOH!" wailed Poppy, KC and Sam in their best spooky voices. Luke and Lucy walked off, muttering.

The rest of the weekend was an unhappy one. They couldn't persuade Olivia and her parents that they had found the secret of the treasure. They decided to give Olivia the rest of the day to calm down. But when the friends went down to Lyon Place the next day, things were no better. The rest of the furniture was being moved out, and everyone was too busy to speak to them. Olivia didn't want them around. "Go play with Luke and Lucy – you like them best," was all she'd say. Nothing that Poppy or KC could say would make her listen.

That afternoon, they sat on the steps of the museum, feeling glum.

"That X must really mark the spot where the treasure is buried," said Poppy, looking over her copy of the map for the hundredth time. "Look, it's marked by a wall. And the cross has oblong shapes at each end, just like the flag on Crossbones Charlie's statue." Poppy had copied every detail of the map before they had run out of the museum.

"It doesn't make any difference now," said Sam. "Olivia said that they're signing the papers to sell the house tomorrow morning."

KC nodded. "And Olivia's dad has locked up the house and there's no way in," she said. KC usually looked on the bright side of things, but, today, even she was feeling gloomy. Dusk was setting in, and the museum was closing.

Mr. Grant came out of the museum and sat down next to them. "Penny for your thoughts?"

Poppy sighed and told him everything. "We were so close. And now the house is going to be sold tomorrow. It was all for nothing – all the clues, and all the exploring."

Mr. Grant patted her on the back. "Don't say that, Poppy. You tried to help a friend, and that's never a bad thing, whatever may happen." He smoothed down his grey moustache and sat thinking for a moment or two. "Mrs. MacArthur will have that passage sealed up," he added. "She doesn't like it

when things interfere with the smooth running of this establishment."

Sam put his head on his hands. "Oh, great. Now we don't even have a secret passage any more."

Mr. Grant's eyes twinkled. "Well, I haven't got around to telling her yet," he said.

The friends looked up at him. "So the passage from the museum is still open?" KC asked.

Mr. Grant nodded slowly. "And I was thinking. If three young people were to turn up here about the same time as yesterday morning, with an accurate map, and a security guard accidentally left the door open . . ."

"Go on," Poppy said.

". . . then there'd be nothing to stop those people from getting in the museum . . ." said Mr. Grant.

"Go on," said KC.

". . . and using the passage to get to some treasure," finished Mr. Grant, looking upwards innocently.

"Huh," said Sam. "Like that's going to happen. I mean, what kind of security guard would – Oh!" Sam looked dumbfounded. "You mean if you left the door open and we went in . . ."

"Quick thinking, silly," said Poppy, giving Sam a hug that he struggled away from. "Would you do that, Mr. Grant? Really?"

Mr. Grant smiled widely. "Let's see, shall we? Say . . . seven o'clock tomorrow morning?"

Poppy, KC and Sam rushed home as quickly as they could. They needed to plan and gather everything they needed for the next morning's treasure hunt. KC phoned her mother, who agreed she could stay over at Poppy's.

Long after Poppy's mum and dad thought the friends were asleep, they were tiptoeing around Poppy's bedroom. Sam checked that the batteries on KC's torch and his penlight were fully charged. Then he checked the alarm for the next day. Poppy was making another copy of the map for emergencies, and making sure they all had

warm clothes for the chilly underground tunnels.
And KC was thinking about how she'd feel, going
back into the dark again for one last time.

"Are you going to be all right, going back down
there?" Poppy asked, sitting on the bed with KC.

KC shrugged. "It's funny," she said. "Since I
tricked Luke and Lucy in the tunnel, I don't feel
like I'm going to be scared again. You know?"

Poppy nodded, and gave her best friend a hug.
"We'll be fine. This time, we'll get that treasure!"

None of the friends thought they would be able
to fall asleep that night. But somehow, before they
knew it, it was morning and Sam's alarm clock
was beeping in his room. He bounced out of bed
and woke up Poppy and KC, and they tumbled
downstairs.

Poppy's dad was sitting in his dressing gown,
eating toast. "You're all up early!" he said.

"Back soon," said Poppy as they rushed out the
door. "Won't be long!"

"I hope you've cleared this with your mother,"
Poppy's dad said, reaching for another piece of
toast.

Chapter 13

Crossbones Charlie's Box

The friends were at the museum a full ten minutes before seven o'clock. Mr. Grant arrived five minutes later. It seemed to take Mr. Grant forever to park his car, get out and walk to the museum gates.

"You three be careful," he said. He handed Poppy a whistle, which she put in her pocket. "If you need help, just blow this and I'll come running. And good luck treasure hunting!"

He went in front of them, switching on lights in the museum as they walked.

Mr. Grant unlocked Mrs. MacArthur's office, and the door to the workshop. Then he left them in the strange, crowded room. There was no time to lose. Poppy climbed over the exhibits to the half-hidden door, and gave it a pull. Just as Mr. Grant had said, it was still open. The steep steps still led downwards, and Poppy shone the torch over them.

"We've got to be extra careful," she called to the others. "Don't forget the broken step!" She stepped carefully onto the first one, turned around and climbed down. Sam and KC followed. KC was only feeling a little more nervous than she had last night.

The way down didn't feel half as long as the way up. When all three of them were on the cold, dusty ground, Poppy pulled out the map. "We go through the hole in the wall, and back to the crossroads," she said. "But this time, we take a different route from last time." The friends climbed through the small hole, and started back down the corridor. They could move much more quickly now that they knew the way. At the crossroads, they stopped. "This way," said Poppy, striding off down the turning. "The treasure's not far off now!"

A few more twists and turns took them into a small chamber. Unlike the brick corridor, the walls were smooth, with no marks on them at all.

"Just think," said Poppy, looking at them. "If we're right, this is the first time anybody's touched the treasure since Crossbones Charlie himself!" It made the three of them feel very strange and solemn, somehow.

Poppy pointed to a wall that looked the same as any other. "Look at the map," she said. "The X is definitely on this wall. We need to search for anything that looks strange."

Poppy started to feel along one side of the wall, Sam felt in the middle, and KC felt along the other side. Poppy ran her fingers down the rough stone. It crumbled a little at her touch, enough for her to be able to scrape a mark into it. But after five minutes of scrabbling, none of them had found anything that felt like a secret compartment.

"Are you sure it's this wall, Poppy?" asked KC.

Poppy nodded. She couldn't understand why they hadn't found anything. "Remember Crossbones Charlie's motto," she said. " 'Never Surrender'. Sam, do you have your screwdriver?"

Sam was rummaging through his bag. "I've got it here somewhere. Here it is!"

"You won't be able to chip the wall away with that," KC said, but Poppy shook her head.

"Maybe we can hear a secret," Poppy said. She tapped the blunt end of the screwdriver on the wall. It made a dull, thudding sound. Poppy moved it slowly across the wall, tapping all the time. "If we hear a hollow sound, that could be it," she explained.

With every tap, the same dull sound came: thud, thud. Poppy had almost reached the bottom of the wall, when –

Thud, thud, tock! They all stopped and Poppy tapped again. No doubt about it, the sound was different!

Poppy turned the screwdriver around and started scraping at the wall. It began to flake away until, first, there was a small hole, and then one large enough to put a hand in, and then a big piece of wall fell away, and a hole the size of a cupboard was revealed!

Poppy shone her torch into the hole. Inside was a small, wooden box. It was a little smaller than a shoebox.

"Open it, Poppy!" whispered KC. Poppy took it with both hands and lifted it out of the hole. She put it on the floor and shone the torch on it. They all gathered around. Poppy lifted the lid, which swung back easily. Inside was an object on a red velvet ribbon. It glinted in the torchlight. Poppy took it out by the ribbon, and the friends saw that it was a round medallion with strange symbols carved into it. And it was made of gold.

For a moment, they couldn't believe it. They just looked at each other. Finally, Poppy broke the silence. "It's true!" she said. "It's all true. Quick – we have to get this to Olivia before the house is sold!"

Poppy put the medallion back into the case, and they made their way back to the crossroads again. "Are we going back to the museum?" asked Sam.

Poppy shook her head. "No time. Olivia said they were signing the papers early today. We have to go back through the tunnels!"

They set off the way they had first entered the underground corridors and, thanks to the map, it wasn't long before they were back at the stone steps that led to the kitchen of Lyon Place.

"I hope they don't mind us coming up this way," said KC.

"I hope they haven't locked the door!" said Sam. But he needn't have worried. When they reached the top of the stairs, the door swung open.

Poppy ran out into the kitchen, through the hall. She pushed the door to the family room open, and saw Olivia's dad about to sign the paper. She ran to him and slammed the case down on top of the paper before his pen could reach it.

"Wait!" she panted. "Treasure!"

It was all she could say before she got her breath back.

Chapter 14

Pirate Gold

For a second, nobody spoke. Poppy looked around the room and saw that Olivia and her mum were standing by the table, looking shocked. Across from the table from Olivia's dad was a man who looked familiar. He had a brown jacket, and an old-fashioned hat was on the table next to him.

Then everyone started talking at once.

"Poppy! Is it true?" Olivia called out, excitedly.

"How did you get in?" said Olivia's dad.

"Where did you get that case?" said Olivia's mum.

"What's the meaning of this?" shouted the man in the brown jacket.

Before she could answer, KC and Sam burst in. Olivia's dad put down his pen. "Did you really get in through a secret passage?" he asked Poppy.

Poppy nodded. But before she could reply, the man in brown interrupted.

Now Poppy knew who he was: Mr. Caxton, the

man with the map whom they'd followed!

"Listen, Mr Lyon. I don't know what these children and their funny box are doing here but, before you find out, would you mind completing our business and signing the house over to me?"

But Olivia's dad wasn't listening. He opened the box and looked at the medallion inside.

"Mr. Caxton," he said, "This looks real to me. But you're the antiques expert. What do you say?"

Mr. Caxton spluttered. "I – I couldn't possibly say. I'm no expert in, um, pirate memorabilia."

"Please, don't listen to him, Mr. Lyon!" Poppy said. "We saw him with the map. He took it from the museum and made a copy of the secret cellar map. Mr. Lyon, he only wants to buy the house to get the treasure!"

"I've never heard such nonsense," snarled Mr. Caxton. "I don't know anything about any treasure! As I've said before, that old map was mysteriously put through my door one morning. I simply returned it to the museum."

Olivia's dad was examining the medallion. "This is really amazing. Did you three find it in the cellars?"

"Yes," said Sam. "In the dark, and everything. Is it – is it worth millions of pounds?"

Everyone leaned in to look at the shining medallion. Olivia's dad held it up and looked at it, frowning.

"No," he said. "It's very old and probably worth a lot of money, but I don't think it's worth enough for us to be able keep the house."

Poppy saw Olivia's face fall. Glancing at Mr. Caxton, she saw him relax, and a false look creep onto his face. The kind of look someone makes when they know something you don't.

"Now you've found your 'treasure', you might as well sign here, Mr. Lyon."

"Wait!" said Poppy. "Why would he still want to buy the house if the treasure was gone? You have to go down to the cellars! Maybe we missed something!"

"I've had enough of you," said Mr. Caxton. "Will you stop interrupting my perfectly normal business deal?"

Olivia's dad looked at Olivia. "What do you think, sweetheart?" he said. "Do you trust them? Yesterday, you said you never wanted to see them again!"

Olivia looked at Poppy, KC and Sam in turn. They couldn't tell what she was thinking.

"I . . . I might have been wrong about them," she said, and smiled.

Olivia's dad stood up. "Then let's go to the cellars," he said.

It wasn't long before Poppy had led them all into the cellars, and down to the wall where they had found the medallion. The grown ups had brought a couple of strong flashlights, and the light spilled everywhere, showing up the cobwebbed corners of the room. Olivia's dad knelt down and poked around the hole.

"Nothing in here," he said. "I guess that all that was left of Crossbones Charlie's treasure was this one piece."

"Of course," said Mr. Caxton. "Houses don't really have thousands of dubloons buried under them. Except in the imaginations of little girls!" and he gave Poppy an unpleasant look.

"No!" said Olivia. "I'm sure it's here. Nobody but Poppy, KC and Sam believed me when I said the treasure was real. So I believe them now!" She took a torch and shone it into the hole. "What's that?" she said. "Look! On the wall at the back. A sort of X shape."

Poppy, KC and Sam looked into the hole. Sure enough, there was a rough cross shape scratched into the bricks.

"X marks the spot," said KC. "I guess that's the X."

"There's something else," said Poppy. "I've seen that before."

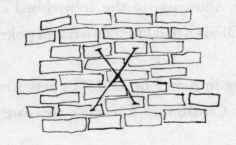

Each end of the cross finished at a brick.

"It's Crossbones Charlie's symbol! Do you remember, on the statue's flag? An X with four oblong shapes." She gathered KC, Sam and Olivia in a huddle and started whispering to them.

"What are they doing?" said Mr. Caxton.

"Olivia's right," said Olivia's mum. "I think it's time we trusted Poppy, too."

The friends came out of the huddle.

"Ready?" asked Poppy, and the others nodded. They all put one hand each into the hole and pressed on the four bricks that were joined by the cross. At first, nothing happened.

"Push harder!" said Poppy, and they strained and strained.

Poppy felt the brick move under her hand – and then it slid right into the wall, falling into a space on the other side. KC and Olivia's bricks followed, and then Sam's brick finally gave way and fell in. As they removed their hands, they saw the whole brick wall tremble.

"Get back, everyone!" said Olivia's mum. "The wall's going to fall in."

They hurriedly backed off and watched as the cement on the wall cracked and an entire section of the wall fell to the ground, raising clouds of red brick dust.

"The four bricks must have been holding the wall together," said Poppy, as she coughed the dust away.

When the air cleared, the friends couldn't believe what they saw. The wall had opened up to a whole other room. And piled high in gleaming heaps, scattered over open chests and scattered all over the floor, were more enormous gold dubloons than they could count!

Everyone except Mr. Caxton shrieked with excitement. Olivia ran and hugged her parents

"We're saved!" she cried. "We're saved! And it's all thanks to you!"

Olivia grabbed Poppy, KC and Sam and gave them a huge hug. "Everything's going to be fine now – right, dad?" she asked.

Olivia's dad nodded, looking dazed. "I think there's more than enough here to ensure we never need to move out of Lyon Place," he said.

Olivia's mum picked up one of the gold coins. "So heavy," she said. "And so many of them."

She turned to Mr. Caxton. She had expected to see him cursing, or even running off, but he was looking at the pile of gold with a strange little smile. He caught her eye. "Oh, well," he said. "I guess I was beaten, fair and square. By three excellent treasure hunters."

"So you were trying to buy the house for the treasure!" Poppy said. "I knew it!"

"I'm afraid so," said Mr. Caxton, who didn't look at all sorry. "You see, I found Crossbones Charlie's diary one day in a pile of old books. It said that he had left a secret map attached to the plans of Lyon Place. So I, um, arranged for the map to be borrowed from the museum, and copied the cellar map. And if it hadn't been for you . . ." he coughed, ". . . wonderful kids, I would have bought the house for next to nothing – with a big pile of treasure underneath! Alas, it was not to be."

"There's one thing I don't understand," said KC. "What about the notes in the museum? The ones that had your address on the back, and led us to the map room?"

"Oh," said Mr. Caxton. "so that's what caused my downfall, is it? Well, I was checking out the museum to make sure all my plans were in place. That's when I realised the map had been moved into a new room. Then, the man I had hired to steal the map showed up. I couldn't be seen talking to him, in case he was caught. So I dropped directions onto the floor, and then passed him a note telling him to follow them." Mr. Caxton looked rather pleased with himself. "The only trouble was," he continued, looking angrier, "that the idiot didn't pick them up after him. Which is why you were able to find them."

Poppy gave him a hard stare. "You're not a very nice person," she said. "You could have told Olivia's dad where the treasure was, but you wanted it for yourself."

Mr. Caxton gave her a fox-like smile. "Maybe I'm not a very nice person," he said. "But I enjoyed this treasure hunt immensely. And now, I fear, I must be gone!" He took a torch and disappeared back down the passage, before anyone could ask him any more awkward questions.

"Guess what, Olivia?" said Olivia's mum. "You'll be able to go back to your old school now!"

Poppy swapped glances with KC. They'd only just got to know Olivia, and now she was going away again. And it was all because they'd managed to find the treasure for her. It didn't seem fair, somehow.

"Hmm," Olivia said. "Mum, I want to stay at school with Poppy and KC. I like it a lot better there!"

Olivia's mum gave her a hug. "You can do whatever you want, darling."

Olivia grinned at Poppy and KC. "I think this is just the start of our fun!"

Sam looked at the huge pile of gold dubloons, as if trying to calculate how many coins there were. Olivia and her parents were looking at the gold and hugging each other. "It certainly tells us one thing," he announced. "Crossbones Charlie must have been a very good pirate."

"You mean a very bad pirate," said Poppy, laughing.

"Whatever," agreed Sam.

**If you've enjoyed meeting Poppy,
KC and Sam, you can try one of these
other exciting books in the
Three Together series.**